Copyright © Joanna Troughton 1977

First published in 1977, reprinted 1978, 1980
Second edition 1986

Blackie and Son Ltd
7 Leicester Place, London WC2H 7PP

British Library Cataloguing in Publication Data
Troughton, Joanna
What made Tiddalik laugh.
I. Title
823'914[J]   PZ7

ISBN 0-216-90431-5

This edition published by
Peter Bedrick Books
2112 Broadway New York, N.Y. 10023

Library of Congress Cataloguing-in-Publication Data
Troughton, Joanna.
  What made Tiddalik laugh.

Summary: Retells the Aboriginal tale about what
happened when the giant frog Tiddalik had such a great
thirst that he drank a lake, a river, and all the
other water he could find until there wasn't a drop of
water left anywhere.
[1. Austalian aborigines-Legends] I. Title.
PZ8.1.T74Wg   1986   398.2' 452789' 09914   [E]   86-1234
ISBN 0-87226-081-X

Printed in Hong Kong

FOLK-TALES OF THE WORLD

What Made Tiddalik Laugh

Retold and illustrated by
Joanna Troughton

Blackie
London

Bedrick/Blackie
New York

Author's note

In central Australia there are frogs which survive
drought by drinking so much water that they
become as round as balls. Then they bury
themselves and wait for the rains to come again.
Maybe this is the origin of the Aborigines' story of
Tiddalik, and how he drank all the
water in the world.

In the Dreamtime, there lived a
giant frog called Tiddalik.
One morning, when he awoke, he
said to himself: "I am s-ooo thirsty,
I could drink a lake!"

And that is what he did!

Then he drank a river.

And then a billabong,

and then a stream.
But Tiddalik was still thirsty.

All day long he searched for water.
All day long he drank.

Slurp, gurgle, slurp.

At last Tiddalik rested.
He had to, for his whole body was swollen with water.
"That's better," he said to himself,
and fell fast asleep.

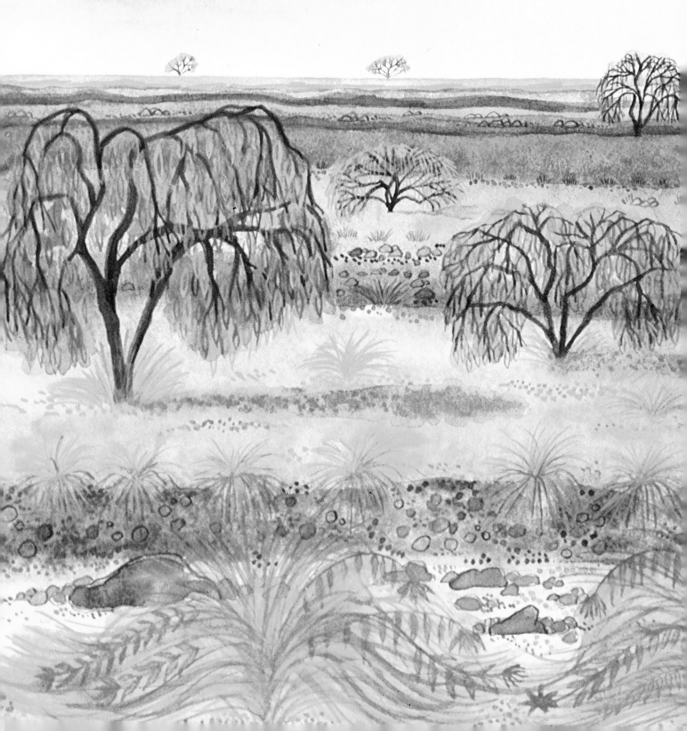

When the sun rose the next morning,
there was not a drop of water to be seen.

The rivers were dry.
The lakes were dry.
The streams were dry.
Leaves withered on the trees.
Flowers wilted in the heat.

"What are we going to do?" asked the birds and the animals.
"Tiddalik has drunk all the water in the world."

"There is only one thing we can do," said a wise old wombat.
"We must make Tiddalik laugh."
The animals were puzzled. "What does he mean?" they asked.
"When Tiddalik laughs," the wombat explained, "he will open
his mouth, and all the water he has drunk will come spilling out."

So the animals decided to hold a Playabout.

They all gathered round Tiddalik.
"Let the Playabout begin!" said the wombat.

Some animals told jokes.

When is water
like a Kangaroo?

When it makes
a spring!

Why do bees hum?

Because they don't
know the words!

But Tiddalik did not laugh.

And some pulled faces.

But Tiddalik did not laugh.

Some played nasty tricks.

But Tiddalik did not laugh.

And some did funny dances.

But Tiddalik did not laugh.

Some sang silly songs.

But still Tiddalik did not laugh.

Deep down in a burrow under the earth, Platypus awoke with a
start. "What is that noise?"

Platypus had not joined in the Playabout, for she belonged to
no animal tribe, and kept herself to herself.

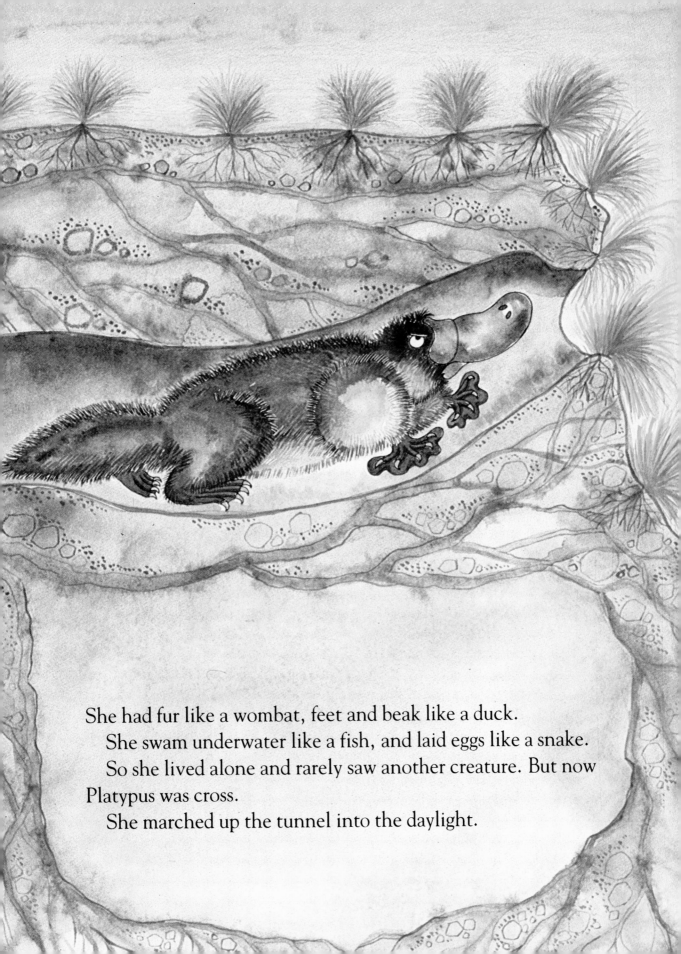

She had fur like a wombat, feet and beak like a duck.

She swam underwater like a fish, and laid eggs like a snake.

So she lived alone and rarely saw another creature. But now Platypus was cross.

She marched up the tunnel into the daylight.

"Excuse me!" Platypus grumbled. "But I was trying to get some sleep!"

Tiddalik's eyes popped out of his head.

He had never seen such a strange animal in all his life.

He began to smile, and a few drops of water fell from his mouth.

And then Tiddalik laughed.

How he laughed!

He roared and guffawed. He chuckled and chortled.

Oh how he laughed!

And from his mouth all the rivers and lakes and streams came swooshing out.

"Well done Platypus!" said the wombat.
"Thank you for making Tiddalik laugh,"
said all the animals.